This book belongs to

....

www.makebelieveideas.com

Written by Rosie Greening.
Illustrated by Lara Ede.

JUST NARWHAL

Lara Ede • Rosie Greening

make
believe
ideas

Narwhal was a whale who thought she had **no skills** at all.

She couldn't **cook** . . .

Recipe

or knit...

or sing...

or even
catch a ball!

Meanwhile, all her **mermaid** friends were skilful as can be.
If they tried out something **new**, they did it **perfectly**.

"**Wow!**" thought Narwhal every day.
"There's nothing they can't do.
But I'm **just Narwhal**,
and I wish that I had **talent** too."

One morning, Star and Coral cried to **Narwhal** in distress:

"Our **art contest** has started, but everything's a **mess!**"

STAR

MARINA

"We need a **judge**," said Coral, "and our time is nearly up. Can **you** judge our paintings and decide who wins this **cup?**"

Narwhal thought,
"I'll get it wrong,"
and quickly shook her head.
She told them, **"I'm just Narwhal –**
I'll find someone else instead."

SANDY

ISLA

CORAL

She asked **Cackle the Clownfish**
to decide which art should win.

ISLA

"The prize goes to the
FUNNIEST!"
said Cackle with a grin.

Narwhal thought,
"That's not enough to win the special prize.
But I'm **just Narwhal**, so I'll check
with someone **big** and **wise**."

She found a **big blue whale** and asked,
"Which painting is the **best?**"

"The
BIGGEST!"
shouted Jumbo.
"**Forget** about the rest!"

"I'm not sure size is **everything**," said Narwhal quietly.
"But since I am **just Narwhal**,
I should check **Shelly** agrees."

Shelly scuttled round the art, but judged them **selfishly**.
The shellfish said, "The **winner** is the one that features . . .

ME!"

MARINA

Narwhal looked around and thought,
"These choices **don't** seem fair.

ISLA

CORAL

MARINA

They **can't** judge on **one thing** alone:
there's **much** more to compare."

Narwhal swam to join her friends.
"**I've let you down!**" she cried.

"You need a **fair** and **honest** judge,
who sees how **hard** you tried."

The mermaids said, "If that's the case,
then **YOU** should judge our art!
To us, you're not '**just Narwhal**',
and we'd **love** you to take part."

Narwhal gave a
nervous smile and said,
"Ok, I'll try!"

STAR

MARINA

ISLA

And she wrote a list of **qualities**
to judge the paintings by.

Narwhal swam around the art,
and **studied** each with care.
She looked at **every** brush stroke
to make sure that she was **fair**.

- Colours ☑
- Theme ☑
- Brushstroke ☐
- Technique ☐
- Effort ☐
- Beauty ☐

SANDY

At last she said, "Each piece of art
is **special** in its way.
But **ONE** ticked every box for me . . .

Star wins first prize today!"

Star held up the shining cup
for **everyone** to see.
Then Coral rushed to Narwhal
and she **hugged** her gratefully.

She said, "You are the **finest** judge
we could have ever found.
You're **fair** and **open-minded**...

the most **just** narwhal around!"

From that day on, **Narwhal** would judge
each contest she could find.

And though she couldn't dance or sing, at last, she didn't **mind**.

She thought,

"My **skills** are hidden –
they're not **obvious** to see.
But just like all the **paintings**,

there is so much **more to me!**"